Chicken Licken

Retold by Alison Hawes

Illustrated by Janet Samuel

RIGBY

One day, a nut fell on Chicken Licken.

"Help!" said Chicken Licken.

"The sky is falling down!

I must run and tell the king!"

Just then, she met Ducky Lucky.
"Quick!" said Chicken Licken.
"We must run and tell the king.
The sky is falling down!"

4

"Quack! Quack!" said Ducky Lucky.

Then they met Henny Penny.
"Quick!" said Chicken Licken.
"We must run and tell the king.
The sky is falling down!"

"Pock! Pock!" said Henny Penny.

Then they met Goosey Loosey.
"Quick!" said Chicken Licken.
"We must run and tell the king.
The sky is falling down!"

"Hiss! Hiss!" said Goosey Loosey.

Then Foxy Loxy saw Chicken Licken,
Ducky Lucky, Henny Penny and
Goosey Loosey – and he licked his lips!

11

"Where are you going in such a rush?"
said Foxy Loxy.
"We're going to see the king!"
said Chicken Licken.

"Come this way, then," said Foxy Loxy.
"This is the quickest way to the king!"

"He's just in here," said Foxy Loxy.

But it was a trick!

It was the way to Foxy Loxy's den!